Dear Parent:
Your child's love of reading starts here!

Every child learns to read in a different way and at his or her own speed. Some go back and forth between reading levels and read favorite books again and again. Others read through each level in order. You can help your young reader improve and become more confident by encouraging his or her own interests and abilities. From books your child reads with you to the first books he or she reads alone, there are I Can Read Books for every stage of reading:

SHARED READING
Basic language, word repetition, and whimsical illustrations, ideal for sharing with your emergent reader

BEGINNING READING
Short sentences, familiar words, and simple concepts for children eager to read on their own

READING WITH HELP
Engaging stories, longer sentences, and language play for developing readers

READING ALONE
Complex plots, challenging vocabulary, and high-interest topics for the independent reader

I Can Read Books have introduced children to the joy of reading since 1957. Featuring award-winning authors and illustrators and a fabulous cast of beloved characters, I Can Read Books set the standard for beginning readers.

A lifetime of discovery begins with the magical words **"I Can Read!"**

Visit www.icanread.com for information
on enriching your child's reading experience.

For Mark Palmer,
Suspicious Trout
—N.D.W.

This one is for Penelope
—F.D.

I Can Read® and I Can Read Book® are trademarks of HarperCollins Publishers.

Hello, Ninja. Goodbye, Tooth!
Text copyright © 2021 by N. D. Wilson
Illustrations copyright © 2021 by Forrest Dickison
All rights reserved. Printed in the United States of America. No part of this book may be used or
reproduced in any manner whatsoever without written permission except in the case of brief quotations
embodied in critical articles and reviews. For information address HarperCollins Children's Books,
a division of HarperCollins Publishers, 195 Broadway, New York, NY 10007.
www.icanread.com

Library of Congress Control Number: 2020949383
ISBN 978-0-06-305618-3 (trade bdg.)—ISBN 978-0-06-305617-6 (pbk.)

Book design by Rachel Zegar

21 22 23 24 25 LSCC 10 9 8 7 6 5 4 3 2 1 ❖ First Edition

HELLO NINJA

Goodbye Tooth

by N. D. Wilson   pictures by Forrest Dickison

HARPER

An Imprint of HarperCollinsPublishers

Uh-oh. Something is wrong
with my tooth.
It is wiggling!

I open my mouth and show Georgie.

She seems excited.

"Wesley!" she yells.

"It is about to come out!

I know just who we need."

"The dentist?" I ask.

Georgie shakes her head.

"No. Guess again."

I think really hard.

Oh! I've got it!

"The tooth fairy?" I ask.

"Wrong!" Georgie laughs.

"Captain Dart!"

I do not know who Captain Dart is.

But the name sounds exciting!

"Captain Dart is an explorer!"
Georgie says.

"And she is a chipmunk."

"Wow!" I say.

"The captain is building a time machine!" Georgie continues. "And teeth are super strong for parts. I bet she will buy your tooth from you. You might get five dollars—or even more!"

This tooth has to come out.

I push it back and forth with my tongue.

"I can help," Georgie says.

"Maybe we can tie your tooth to a
toy truck with this string."

This seems like a good idea to me!

Trucks are strong.

"Let's try it, Georgie." I say.

Will our plan work?

My loose tooth flies out of my mouth.

Oh no! Is it lost?

"I don't see it anywhere," I say.

"Maybe I won't get any money after all."

"Don't give up," Georgie says.
"We just need to look harder."
"Hmm. Maybe we just need to
be ninjas!" I say.

"Hello, ninjas!"

"Yes, hello."

Okay. That's much better.

It's Kuma!

Thank goodness she is here to help!

"What brings you three to the land

of Ninja?" Kuma asks.

"Are you on a quest?"

"I need to find my lost tooth," I say.

"Wesley is going to sell it to Captain Dart!" Georgie says.

"The chipmunk?" Kuma asks. "She is very clever."

"I'm going to buy amazing things
with the money," I say.
"Like a race car for my dad,
or a sailboat for my mom.
Or maybe I will buy a castle!"

Kuma laughs.

"Captain Dart might not pay you enough for castles or race cars!"

"Look, Wesley!" Georgie yells.

"There she is!

And she found your tooth!"

Uh-oh! The captain is in trouble!

A magpie is chasing her!

"Leave me alone!" Captain Dart yells at the bird.

"Kuma, follow that bird!" I say.

"Ninjas to the rescue!" Georgie shouts.

The magpie is fast, but so are we!

We all chase it through the jungle,

with Captain Dart following behind us.

The magpie hits a tree branch and drops my tooth onto a sleeping snake!

We will have to be very sneaky ninjas or the big snake will wake up.

Ninjas can be very quiet,
even upside down!

And chipmunks have sneaky little paws
that are just right for this job!

We did it!

We found my tooth!

"This would be perfect in my time machine!" Captain Dart says.

"But I am all out of money right now."

"You can keep it," I say.

"I will grow another one. And you did find it first."

"Finders keepers!" Georgie says.

Captain Dart looks very happy.

And that makes me happy.

If she needs anything else,

I will try to find it for her.

Besides, I do not need five dollars
or a castle to be happy.

I have friends like Georgie and Pretzel and a flying dragon.

Maybe someday, Captain Dart will let me ride in her time machine!

Until then, I will imagine my tooth going on all sorts of adventures.